# MOOSHKA

## A QUILT STORY

To Karla Paschkis
—*J. P.*

Ω

Published by
PEACHTREE PUBLISHERS
1700 Chattahoochee Avenue
Atlanta, Georgia 30318-2112

www.peachtree-online.com

Text and illustrations © 2012 by Julie Paschkis

Illustrations created in India ink and gouache on 100% rag archival watercolor
paper.
Title typeset in Dieter Steffmann's Kalenderblatt Grotesk; text typeset in
International Typeface Corporation's Fenice by Aldo Novarese.

Printed and manufactured in August 2012 by Tien Wah Press in Malaysia
10 9 8 7 6 5 4 3 2

Library of Congress Cataloging-in-Publication Data
Paschkis, Julie.
  Mooshka, a quilt story / written and illustrated by Julie Paschkis.
    p. cm.
  Summary: Karla's quilt Mooshka tells her stories about the pieces of fabric that Mooshka is
made from, but when Karla's baby sister is born, Mooshka falls silent until Karla overcomes
her jealousy and shares Mooshka with the baby.
          ISBN 978-1-56145-620-8 / 1-56145-620-9
            [1. Quilts--Fiction. 2. Sisters--Fiction. 3. Babies--Fiction. 4. Sharing--Fiction.]
              I. Title.
                PZ7.P2686Mo 2012
                  [E]--dc23
                                            2011020463

# MOOSHKA
## A QUILT STORY

WRITTEN AND ILLUSTRATED BY

# JULIE PASCHKIS

Ω
PEACHTREE
ATLANTA

Karla had an unusual quilt.

She called it Mooshka.

Mooshka kept her warm on cold nights
and had a nice toasty smell.
Its colors and patterns made her room bright
and cheery even on the rainiest of days.

If there was something scary under the bed, it snuggled tight around her and made her feel safe.

But that wasn't why Karla's quilt was unusual.

Mooshka was different

because it could talk to her.

At bedtime Mooshka always said,

"Sweet dreams."

First thing in the morning

Mooshka might say, "Pancakes."

Karla's grandmother had made the quilt
from scraps of old fabric that she called
*schnitz.* As she sewed the pieces together,
she told Karla stories.

If Karla couldn't sleep in the middle of the night, she would put her hand on a schnitz and it would tell her its story.

Mooshka would go on and on until Karla was fast asleep.

Each bit of fabric had a different way
of speaking.

The yellow schnitz spoke in a soft cottony
voice. "I was a tablecloth at Grandmother's
farmhouse, which was all right, especially
when something sweet spilled. I was glad
to be useful. But once when your Aunt
Marjorie was a girl, she made me into a tent
and told fortunes beneath my golden folds.
Now that was glorious!"

The blue schnitz had a sturdy voice.
"Grandpa Will lived on the other side of
the mountain. He walked for three days
over the hills and asked Lily Jane to marry
him. I was the kerchief around his neck.

When he reached the apple orchard, he went
right up to her and said, 'I'm yours, now or never.'
And he wiped his brow with me and didn't leave
until she said yes."

The red schnitz spoke in a cheery tone.
"When your mother was just your age,
she thought she could fly. She made me
into a cape and jumped out of the cherry tree.
Such fun—I fluttered and flapped in the wind.

She broke her toe but that wasn't my fault."

Karla loved listening to the stories.

Sometimes she would talk about something

the quilt had told her and her mother would say

"Now, how did you know that?"

One day a little white crib was moved
into Karla's room. Hannah was in the crib.

That night Mooshka didn't say a word,
not even "Sweet dreams."
Karla could think of many words.

*Unfair.*

*Stinky.*

*My room.*

But Mooshka was silent.

Night after night Karla would put her
hand on a schnitz hoping for a story,
but Mooshka kept quiet.

Karla tried to start the stories.
"Do you remember when you were
the curtains in Dad's old sailboat?"
"Do you remember when you were
a Halloween costume for the dog?"

But Mooshka still didn't speak.

Once, in the middle of the night, Hannah started to cry. She cried and cried.

Karla squeezed her eyes shut and put her
hands over her ears, but she could still
hear Hannah crying.

Karla got out of bed. She picked up her quilt
and carried it to the crib. She puffed Mooshka
in the air and let it float gently down on Hannah.

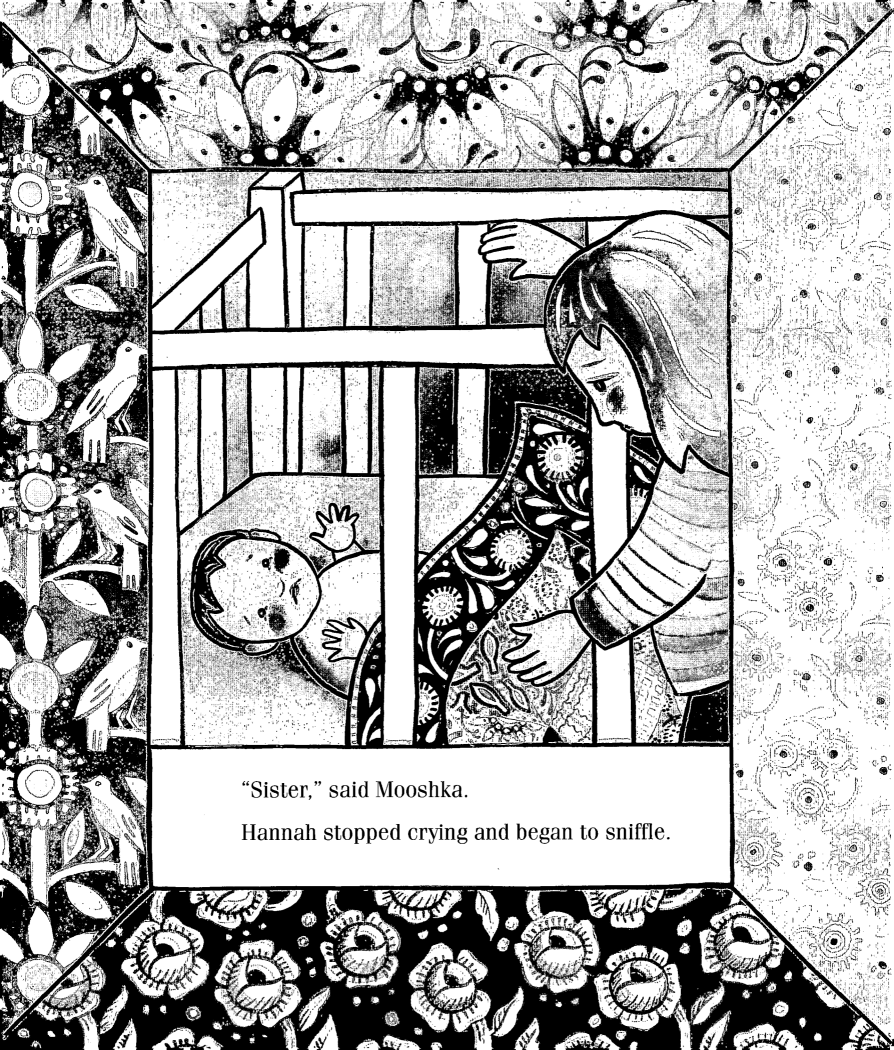

"Sister," said Mooshka.

Hannah stopped crying and began to sniffle.

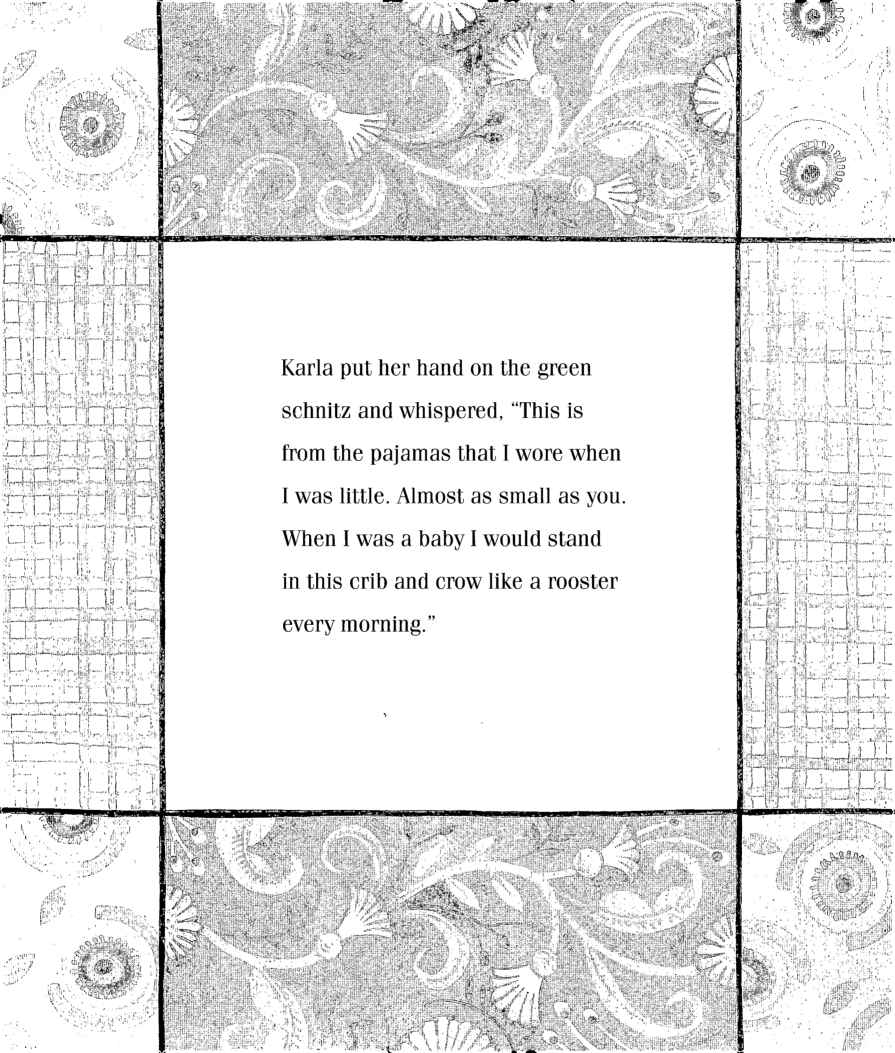

Karla put her hand on the green
schnitz and whispered, "This is
from the pajamas that I wore when
I was little. Almost as small as you.
When I was a baby I would stand
in this crib and crow like a rooster
every morning."

Hannah was quiet

and Mooshka was quiet

and Karla went on and on.